THE THUMBTACK DANCER

BY LESLIE TRYON   ILLUSTRATED BY JAN SPIVEY GILCHRIST

PRESS

CARRBORO, NORTH CAROLINA

For Ashley Bryan,
whose creativity and love have overcome all obstacles
— and inspired Gus to dance.
LESLIE TRYON

Especially for Susan Valdina.
Thank you for being my dear sister in love.
Acknowledgement to my model Jahkil Neem Jackson,
Thanks for tapping through this book.
JAN SPIVEY GILCHRIST

Just like yesterday and the day before,
Gus *KICKED* out of bed,
        LACED-UP his thumbtack sneakers
        and did his
          teeth-brushing dance.

Next he did his
bed-making dance,
and then his
getting-dressed dance.

His mama knew Gus was up because she could hear, the
tip-a-tap, rap-a-slap, flap-a-dap
thumbtack rhythms through the kitchen ceiling.

Just like yesterday and the day before,

Gus went *SLIIII-DING* down the hallway
on his slippery thumbtacks. He
wooshhhh-ed
past his mama and out the kitchen door.

Then he
flip-flap, skip-rapped
down the front steps
BACKWARDS!

Just like yesterday and the day before,

Gus riffed,
slap-a-dee-dap, slap-a-dee-dap

down the sidewalk, and right up to
the big red door of the dance studio.

He knock!
knock!
KNOCKED!
on the big red
dance studio door,
and when the
tall skinny
dance teacher
with the cane
opened the door,
Gus went
into his
Watch-this!
dance,
just as he
had done
yesterday
and
the day
before.

"You're just a sidewalk dancer," the annoyed dance
teacher said.
    "I told you yesterday
        and I told you the day before,
thumbtacks are absolutely **not allowed**
on these hardwood floors.
You won't get through this door until you have
real tap shoes."

Gus couldn't afford real tap shoes
    yesterday or the day before.
He thought that he might not be able to
    afford real tap shoes
        tomorrow or the day after either.

Gus decided to do some serious thinking
about his situation. He was doing his
serious-thinking dance
when . . .

. . . a mother pushing a stroller
with a cranky, crying baby inside
stopped to watch him.
When Gus danced around the stroller, that
cranky baby giggled.

The mother was so happy to see her baby giggle,
        she gave Gus
                a coin!

Gus bowed to the mother —
a bow is how dancers say
thank you!

Gus did some **tippy-taps** way up on his toes,

which grew into a

getting-an-idea dance.

He put his cap on the sidewalk and

started right away on his

earning-money-to-buy-tap-shoes dance.

He
slip-slapped
and
rap-a-flapped
his
happy dance
all over
that
sidewalk.

Some people would stop
to watch Gus dance for a minute
and then they'd put some coins
in his cap.
Others didn't even stop
but they tossed in a coin
as they walked by.

He twirled, he spun; he *JUMPED* high
into the air and made the most amazing
flam-a-diddle, par-a-diddle
drum rhythms with his feet.

A crowd gathered around.

They clapped and they stomped to the beat of Gus' rhythms. That crowd was having a really good time.

Gus could see that there were a lot of coins in his cap, maybe even enough to buy some **real tap shoes!**

Today must be my lucky day, he thought as he danced.

"Go thumbtack dancer!
Go!" someone shouted.

"Will you be dancing here again
  tomorrow?" another asked.

"And the day after tomorrow?"
  someone else wanted to know.

All that clapping and

    all the wonderful things the people

        said about him made Gus feel

            famous . . .

He did a big **thank-you bow** and held it

    for as long as the people kept clapping.

Gus did his
happy dance
all the way to the dance studio.
He knock!
knock!
KNOCKED!
on that big red door.

When the dance teacher opened the door,
Gus broke into his
I-did-it dance!
He told him he had
earned enough coins
to buy a pair of
real tap shoes!

"Will you buy them today?" the dance teacher asked.

"Not today," Gus said, "but . . .